We've got him all the stuff he'll need,

his basket, collar, bowl and lead.

At first, a puppy's scared and shy,

So Mummy's careful. So am I.

We give this special food to him.

It helps him grow. He tucks right in!

I hold him gently so he knows

I love him – and he licks my nose.

And when he wakes up in the morning,

How he stretches! See him yawning!

Soon he's ready for the day,

And all he wants to do is play.

He nuzzles at my ears and feet.

It tickles, but it's very sweet.

I stroke him and I scratch his tum.

He wags his tail, which means "what fun"!

He wants to nibble everything,

Like papers, clothes and bits of string.

It's not so funny when he chews

The laces off my daddy's shoes!

He seems to wee just everywhere,

But soon he'll learn, so we don't care.

He loves a visit to the park,

And sometimes bravely tries his bark.

He sniffs the flowers, grass and trees

And chases butterflies and bees.

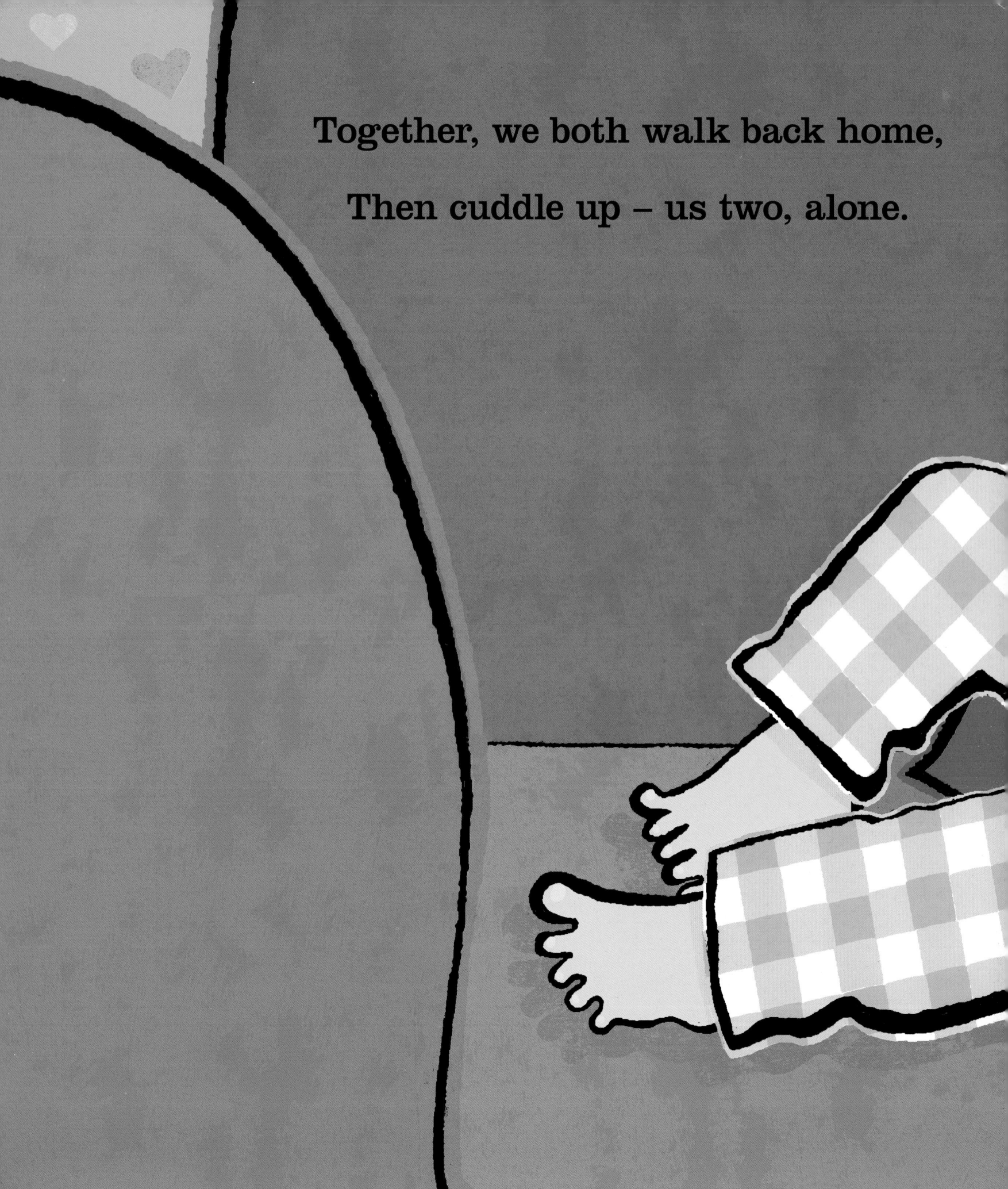

Together, we both walk back home,

Then cuddle up – us two, alone.

And when he's tired and lolls his head

We put him in his cosy bed,

And watch his little sleeping form,

All soft and still . . .

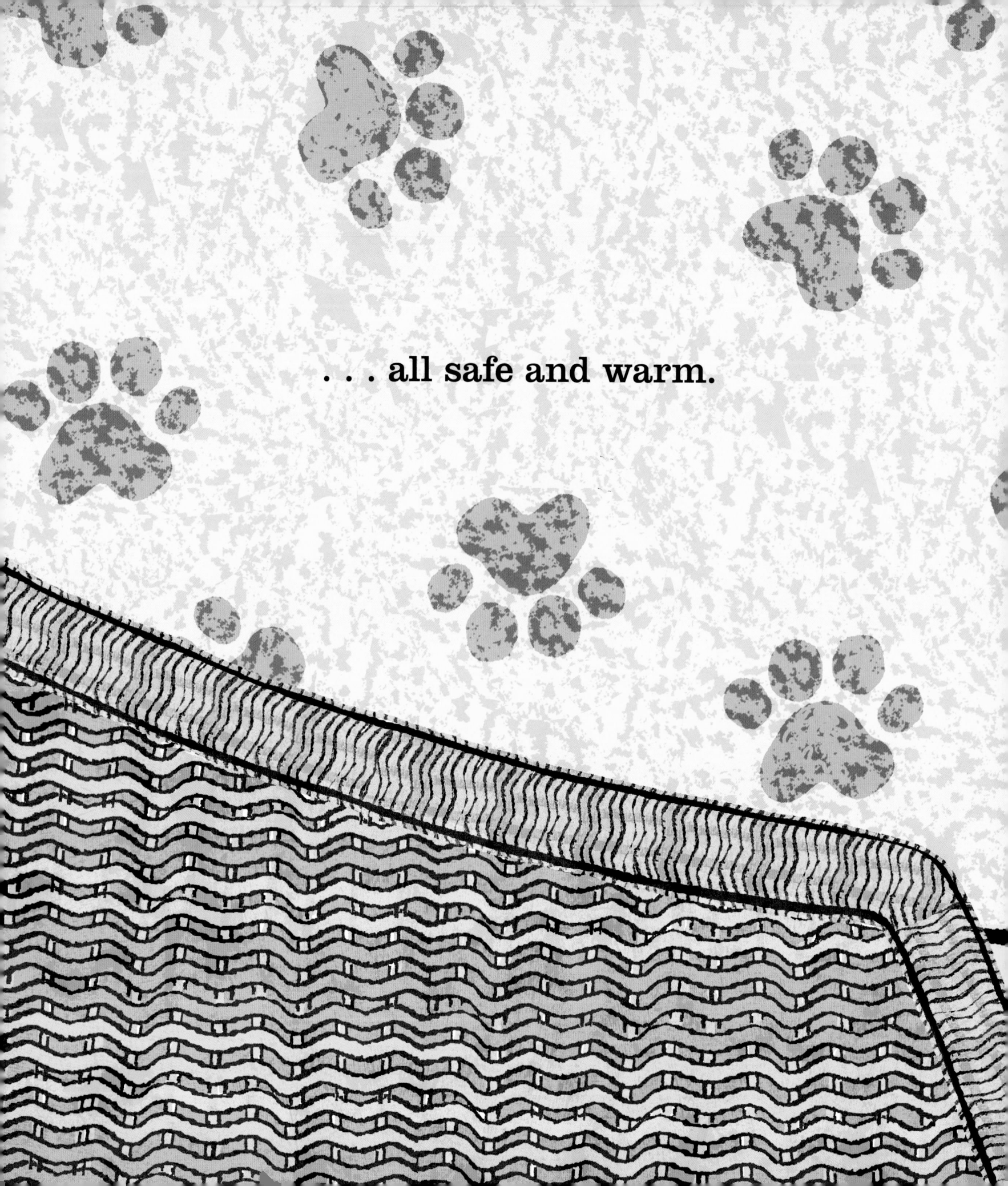

. . . all safe and warm.

For Finn, Ralph and Kate
with love, Giles

For Buzz Wells
and Ruby Gerrard
with love, Emma xx

ORCHARD BOOKS

Carmelite House

50 Victoria Embankment

London EC4Y 0DZ

First published in 2015 by Orchard Books

ISBN 978 1 40833 814 8

Text © Giles Andreae 2015

Illustrations © Emma Dodd 2015

A CIP catalogue record for this book
is available from the British Library.

1 3 5 7 9 10 8 6 4 2

Printed in China

Orchard Books

An imprint of Hachette Children's Group

Part of The Watts Publishing Group Limited

An Hachette UK Company

www.hachette.co.uk

FSC
www.fsc.org

MIX
Paper from
responsible sources
FSC® C104740